Hot Dog
and the
Talent Competition

by Paul Stewart
illustrated by Nick Ward

PICTURE WINDOW BOOKS
Minneapolis, Minnesota

Editor: Jill Kalz
Page Production: Brandie Shoemaker
Art Director: Nathan Gassman
Associate Managing Editor: Christianne Jones

First American edition published in 2007 by
Picture Window Books
5115 Excelsior Boulevard
Suite 232
Minneapolis, MN 55416
877-845-8392
www.picturewindowbooks.com

Library of Congress Cataloging-in-Publication Data
Stewart, Paul, 1955–
Hot Dog and the talent competition / by Paul Stewart ; illustrated by
Nick Ward.
p. cm. — (Read-it! chapter books)
Summary: When Ella enters her dog, Hot Dog, in the school fair's
competition, she finds that her pet has a creative approach to the commands
she gives him.
ISBN-13: 978-1-4048-3129-2 (library binding)
ISBN-10: 1-4048-3129-0 (library binding)
[1. Dogs—Fiction. 2. Contests—Fiction.] I. Ward, Nick, 1955– ill. II. Title.
PZ7.S84975Ho 2006
[Fic]—dc22   2006027280

Table of Contents

Chapter One

"What am I going to do?" worried Ella. "It's 11 o'clock, already!"

Ella was at the park with her dog, Hot Dog. It was where she always went when she had a problem.

The School Fair started in two hours, and Ella still didn't know what to sign up for. The art show? The music competition? A track and field event?

"Woof! Woof!" Hot Dog barked.

All of a sudden, Ella was struck by a brilliant idea. Of course! Why hadn't she thought of it before? The dog talent competition!

She looked around. Hot Dog, still barking loudly, was racing toward a muddy puddle.

"Here, Hot Dog," Ella called.

"And miss all of that wonderful mud?" thought Hot Dog. "You must be joking!"

"Hot Dog!" shouted Ella, chasing after him. "You have to look your best this afternoon. There's a dog talent compe—"

Too late. Hot Dog had jumped into the puddle and was already rolling in thick mud.

Ella sighed. "Now I'll have to give you a bath," she said.

"Nonsense," thought Hot Dog. "If I splash around a little bit, I'll end up as clean as anything. Anyway, I don't want to enter a dog talent comp-a … comp-a-tishoo …"

"Hot Dog!" bellowed Ella.

Hot Dog turned. Ella looked upset, and he hated that. He trotted over to her to make her feel better.

He jumped up to give her a big, slurpy kiss.

"Yuck!" Ella shouted. "Get down, Hot Dog!"

Hot Dog cocked his head and stared at Ella, puzzled. There were black marks all over her T-shirt and jeans. Sometimes that girl could be so messy!

"If we are going to win that comp-a-tishoo," he thought, "then you'll have to look your best, too."

Chapter Two

Hot Dog hopped into the tub, and Ella started to give him a bath. He hadn't always been called Hot Dog. A year ago, Mom and Dad had taken Ella to the local animal shelter. Ella and the puppy had looked at each other, and it was love at first sight.

"He's the one I want," said Ella. "I'll call him Sebastian."

Time passed, and Sebastian grew—or rather, most of him did.

Although he had a proud head, a powerful body, and a long, slender tail, Sebastian's legs remained stubby and short.

"He looks like a barrel on four sticks," said Dad. "Something's just not right."

"Dad, don't," said Ella. "You'll hurt his feelings."

Mom called the shelter and discovered that, yes, Sebastian was a mixed breed. His father was a Labrador retriever, but his mother was a dachshund.

"He looks like a hot dog!" Dad exclaimed. And the name stuck. From that moment on, Sebastian was Hot Dog.

"Good dog," Ella murmured as she rubbed Hot Dog's clean, wet fur with a towel. "You look great." She tickled his ears. "We'll win that competition for sure—as long as you're a good dog."

Hot Dog wagged his tail. When Ella was happy, he was happy.

"Good dog?" he thought, "I'm going to be the best dog! You'll see."

Chapter Three

Ready at last, Ella and Hot Dog left the house. Outside the school, other dogs were arriving with their owners. Hot Dog knew the dogs from the dog park. Ella knew the children from school.

Tyrone, a pudgy, short-haired bulldog, stood with a pudgy, short-haired bully named Luke.

There was Beth, a jumpy spaniel,
with a jumpy girl named Lisa.

There was Scamp, a scruffy terrier,
with a scruffy boy named Terry.

Hot Dog looked up at Ella. Did he
and she look alike? Certainly, they
both had sandy hair and brown eyes.
But if Ella really wanted to look like
him, then she would have to walk on
her knees.

Just then, Mrs. Everett, the school secretary, appeared with her tiny poodle, Mimi. They really did look like each other!

Hot Dog sniffed. "Silly creature," he thought, "and as for Mimi, she's a disgrace to all dogs!"

The School Fair was in full swing as Ella and Hot Dog picked their way through the crowds. Hot Dog was in a hurry.

He had smelled something delicious and was tugging Ella around the fair. Finally he found it. A hot dog vendor!

"Yum, those smell good," said Ella, counting her money. "But I have only enough money for the talent competition fee."

"Don't worry about it," thought Hot Dog. "I'll get you one."

He was about to jump up and grab the nearest hot dog in his mouth when Ella tugged his leash.

"Come on, Hot Dog," she said.

Hot Dog tugged back.

"Hot Dog!" said Ella sharply.

Hot Dog stopped pulling and whined, "Party pooper."

Just then, a voice crackled over the loudspeaker: "Will all dog owners please make their way to the school field? This is the last call for the talent competition."

Chapter Four

Ella paid her entry fee and entered Hot Dog in the competition. He was given a number—number 13. Ella hoped it wasn't unlucky 13!

"Now, be good," she told Hot Dog as they took their place at the end of the line.

"Of course," thought Hot Dog. He glanced at the other dogs. "Anything they can do, I can do much better!"

A woman with "Judge" pinned to her jacket stood up. "Good afternoon," she said. "I see you all have lovely dogs. But there can be only one winner of the cup and cash prize. We are about to find out who that lucky dog is."

"Me, of course," thought Hot Dog.

"The talent competition is divided into three parts: Jump, Fetch, and Stay," the judge went on. "The first part will take place over here." She pointed to a series of numbered gates. "Competitor number one, please begin."

Lisa led Beth forward. The jumping began.

Beth quickly jumped over the gates in the right order.

"She's very good," said Ella.

"Humph!" thought Hot Dog. "Boring! I can do much, much better than that."

Soon it was Hot Dog's turn. Ella pointed to the first gate.

"Jump, boy," she said.

"Jump? With my legs?" thought Hot Dog. "Not likely." He had planned a special routine of his own.

He scurried under gate number one, skidded around gates two, three, and four in a snaking movement, and then shot through gate five.

Already he could hear the crowd laughing. They loved him!

With a joyful bark, Hot Dog jumped over gate six and leapt onto gate seven, where he balanced for a brief, shining moment.

Then he threw himself into Ella's waiting arms.

Ella put Hot Dog down on the ground. Her head was pounding. Her face was red.

"He did manage one jump," said the judge kindly.

"Yes," thought Hot Dog proudly. "On top of everything else, I even managed a jump. With my performance, we're sure to win!"

The second event—Fetch—tested how well and how fast the dogs could bring things back. Once again, the other dogs did just as they were told.

But Hot Dog had decided to make the tricks more interesting.

"Number 13," the judge said at last. "It's your turn."

Ella and Hot Dog stepped forward to the sound of laughter and whistles. "It's that funny dog with the short legs," someone said.

Hot Dog bowed. "I'm going to enjoy this," he thought.

For the first trick, Hot Dog was supposed to run and fetch a rubber ring when Ella gave the command.

He got ready. He got set.

Ella raised her arm and tossed
the ring across the field. "Fet—" she
began. But Hot Dog was already
dashing after it.

"I'll show them," he thought. "Any
fool can carry a rubber ring in his
mouth. I'll race back with it balanced
on my nose."

As the ring rolled along the ground,
Hot Dog put his nose through ...

… and got it stuck.

"Whoops," thought Hot Dog. He tried to get it off—with his front paws, his back leg, and by spinning around and around.

But the ring wouldn't budge.
The crowd went wild.
"Here, boy," he heard Ella calling.
"Come HERE!"

"Wait a minute," he thought. "If I can just get my … "

The next instant, Ella yanked the ring roughly from his nose. "I thought I told you to be good, Hot Dog," she hissed. "Everyone is laughing at us."

Hot Dog paused. "Are you sure?" he thought uneasily.

He looked around at the sea of faces. They were jeering and pointing. Ella was right. They were laughing at him. He hung his head. He had made a fool of himself—and Ella. Again!

He remembered the time he'd gotten stuck halfway through the doggie door ... the time he'd dug a hole in the garden so deep he couldn't get out ... and that awful day when he'd gotten trapped inside the pipe that workmen were laying in front of the house. It had taken three hours to pull him free.

But this time, he'd gone too far. Ella was crying.

"I'm sorry, Ella," he thought. "What can I do to cheer you up?" His nose twitched. Of course! He knew exactly what to do.

"Hot Dog!" Ella called through her tears as he bounded across the grass. "Where are you going now?"

The crowd laughed louder than ever. Ella stood there, wishing the ground would swallow her up.

"Here he comes again!" someone shouted a moment later. "Look at him go!"

Back in the field, Hot Dog dashed over to Ella and dropped something on the grass.

He stood there, ears perked and tail wagging. Ella looked down. A hot dog lay at her feet.

"It's for you," thought Hot Dog. "A present—to cheer you up."

Ella was mad. "Hot Dog, come on!" she said, grabbing him by the collar. "First, I have to apologize for that hot dog you stole. Then, we're going home."

"Home?" thought Hot Dog. "We can't go home." He sat down. "We haven't won the comp-a-tishoo yet."

"Come on!" said Ella, pulling him with all her strength.

But Hot Dog would not budge.

"You are HOPELESS!" Ella shouted, kicking the hot dog angrily.

Hot Dog watched his present for Ella bounce over the grass.

"What a waste of good food!" he thought sadly. "What was wrong with it, anyway?"

Chapter Five

The hot dog landed close to Beth. She was about to bite into the treat that had appeared from nowhere when Tyrone snapped at it.

But Scamp wanted the hot dog, too. He leapt onto the bulldog's back and bit his ear. Tyrone yelped with pain and snarled at Mimi.

"Keep that dog away from my Mimikins!" Mrs. Everett squealed, lashing out with her umbrella.

Scamp spotted his chance, snatched the hot dog, and swallowed it in one great, greedy gulp.

All at once, the field exploded with frantic barking. Twelve of the 13 dogs in the competition went crazy—and no one could stop them.

A beagle leapt at a greyhound.
Two shaggy dogs began chasing
a Pekinese. A Dalmatian dashed
between everyone's legs.

The crowd whooped and cheered.
This show was even better than the
one the funny short-legged dog had
put on.

"Please! Please! Control your dogs!" the judge bellowed.

Soon everyone was calling out a dog name.

43

Ella was the only one who wasn't shouting. For once, Hot Dog was as good as gold.

"Dreadful behavior," he sniffed. "You wouldn't catch me being so—"

There was an ear-splitting yell.

The judge had raced over to control the dogs, and they had made her trip.

Excitedly, they all piled on top of her and licked her with their long, slobbery tongues.

"Get off of me!" she roared. "Ugh! Stop that!"

Ella couldn't stand by a moment longer. "STAY!" she told Hot Dog.

Hot Dog saw that she meant it and immediately obeyed.

Ella marched across the grass and began pulling the dogs off the judge.

The judge scrambled to her feet. She looked furious.

"Never, in 25 years," she said fiercely, "have I seen anything like it. You're all out of the competition!"

"But—" Ella began.

"Not you, my dear," the judge said with a smile. She pointed at Hot Dog, who was still waiting for Ella. "The winner of the dog talent competition is number 13, Hot Dog. Well done!"

Ella could hardly believe her ears. They'd won! Still dazed, she walked over to Hot Dog, proudly carrying the winner's silver cup and a crisp $10 bill.

"We won!" she said.

"Of course," thought Hot Dog, glad to see Ella looking happy once more. "Didn't I tell you?"

"Come on, Hot Dog," said Ella. "Let's both have a hot dog. We've earned it."

Look for More *Read-it!* Chapter Books

Looking for a specific title? A complete list
of *Read-it!* Chapter Books is available on our Web site:
www.picturewindowbooks.com